About the Author

I have a background in nursing, both in hospital and community settings, and have a keen interest in the psychology of the human mind. This is my first adult psychological thriller, and I have enjoyed writing about this interesting and in-depth subject. I am an established author with Olympia publishers, having had my first two children's books published in the last two years. I began writing my next book with the same excitement and motivation as before. Please enjoy.

D.G. Hills

Dreams, Wishes and a Ticket to Hell

Olympia Publishers
London

www.olympiapublishers.com
OLYMPIA PAPERBACK EDITION

A CIP catalogue record for this title is available from the British Library.

ISBN: 978-1-80074-880-4

This is a work of fiction.
Names, characters, places and incidents originate from the writer's
imagination. Any resemblance to actual persons, living or dead, is
purely coincidental.

First Published in 2023

Olympia Publishers
Tallis House
2 Tallis Street
London
EC4Y 0AB

Printed in Great Britain

Dedication

I dedicate this book to all the vulnerable people who have travelled through life with challenge, circumstance and negative impact. This book solely depicts how relationships can change the paths we take in life, and how emotionally damaged we can ultimately become.

Acknowledgements

Thank you to all who are in my life and have always believed in me, even through the darkest, and most challenging, of times.

Clementine Fosdyke was an extraordinary woman. She had lived in the village of Gladbury upon Tressle all of her life.

She was a rather formidable woman who had looked after her mother and father until their recent demise. People would often see her riding her bike through the village and smiling at everyone as she cycled past rather drearily, almost as if she weren't enjoying the ride.

A tall thin lady who looked much older than her fifty-two years, she dressed rather plainly and had very long sharp horse-like features. Not the most attractive of women it has to be said but Clementine had a heart of gold and everyone loved her. She had worked in the local library for years now and also did some voluntary work with the local community WI, baking, sewing and knitting for various events in the village.

Her mother and father had been seen to protect her all her life from the horrors of the modern-day world and this, it has to be said, had absolutely impacted on her ability to communicate and socialise with people or indeed spread her wings (dare we say!) outside the village. The very thought would have horrified Clementine. She had been a good daughter, an excellent carer and had it not been for her 'saviour' coming into her life, she would have been totally alone. Her job at the library had helped her through the toughest of times and she so enjoyed going to work three days a week where she could speak to people and she was able to raise the slightest hint of a smile.

Now Clementine had been born with a very special gift. No one had known or did know about her 'gift'. Her mother had known about it from a very young age and had guided her on how best to cope with such an 'affliction'. Or was it a curse? Clementine could never decide which as it had brought her lots of sleepless nights and pain throughout the years. Her gift? Well she could hear what people were thinking. Now that might not sound too bad, but of course some of those thoughts were very dark, perverted and horrifying. She had always found such a gift difficult to deal with as she could be standing talking to someone, when out of the blue, there would be every thought and feeling being clearly communicated to her from the person standing in front of her. Oh it had been a curse and with the support of her mother Clementine had been able to manage her gift without causing anyone any distress or pain. But of course, her mother wasn't here anymore and Clementine was finding it increasingly difficult to live with such a curse.

She could also feel herself changing, she was becoming most intolerant about the thoughts she was hearing. Clementine was becoming very tired of being such a goody two shoes. The villagers didn't think she knew they were talking about her. "Oh, did you see Clementine at the community picnic? She looks so drab and boring," they would say throwing their heads back and laughing loudly.

"Oh she's a bit of a soul, always on her own and no one to go home to, poor soul."

This incensed Clementine, little did they know that she knew *everything* about *everyone*. No, *they* were the poor souls and not her. The facade throughout her life had fooled everyone, even her at times, and this would become horrifyingly clear to all who were around her.

The house that Clementine lived in was a picturesque cottage in the middle of the woods. All you could hear were the birds in the trees. It was so very, very, quiet. She loved it. Her quaint house had a cellar which normally held her father's homemade ale but was empty now. She often felt a rather dark and negative force in the cellar, she wasn't afraid, in fact, she quite liked it and she would often sit down there for hours. Clementine began to think how she could now use the cellar. Pity it's sitting here and not being used, she would say as she stroked her face with her long skeletal fingers whilst having some rather dark thoughts herself. Now how best to use it she thought? Someone could be in this cellar for years and no one would know. Someone could suffer terrible pain down here and no one would know, someone could indeed die down here and no one would ever find them. Oh dear, she couldn't believe she was having such horrifying and dark thoughts, but you know there was a part of her that was feeling an emotion she had never felt before. Excitement. A tingling sensation was running through her body and she knew she had begun a terrifying and exciting journey. More importantly, Clementine had recently met someone who had totally changed her life. This person was about to take her on an adventure like no other so she knew she would never be alone again.

And this, it has to be said, had urged Clementine to change. She craved a new look, a new her so she had made the decision to tart herself up! She put some make-up on, something she would never normally do, and this wasn't any old make-up. It had once belonged to her mother. Clementine styled her hair differently (just like her mother's), and put her mother's clothes on. These particular clothes had been much more with it than her own. She had decided to throw her bike over a hill and into a ditch, shrieking with delight as she did so and walked into the village, a confident and different person.

Heads started to turn, people couldn't believe their eyes. She walked with her head held high, her grey hair flowing in the wind, her horse-like features no more as her make-up complemented her face. Her skirt was a bit shorter than usual, well, let's be honest, it was her mother's skirt, and she of course, was the biggest slut ever to walk our pleasant and wonderful earth! She chuckled to herself. People were looking at her and it felt bloody great.

After her very public exhibition, she returned to the cottage and carefully looked around. This place she had lived in all of her life, now, meant nothing to her. This new and amazing person who had entered her life had made her look at things very differently. She was her advocate, soulmate and heroine. Clementine started to reflect on her life when she was sitting in the cellar, she thought back to the times she had spent with her mother and father when she was young and how very awful growing up with them both had been. Her mother had been a whore and her father a rather pitiful excuse of a man. She would often lie in bed and listen to the drunken rantings of her mother, and of course, the traffic of men who would come and go from the cottage. She remembered her mother shouting, "Clementine, get out your bed! Come and meet..." whatever the bloody stupid name the man had (that's if her mother could remember). "Come and sing, come and dance." And there Clementine would be forced to perform for her mother and her latest conquest. Her mother reeking of booze and the man all over her like some kind of wild animal. She would only have been five or six at the time but she could still smell that awful stench of booze, cigarettes and sex. Oh yes, even at such a young age she knew that was the smell. Sometimes the men would carry her through from her bedroom to perform, she could remember getting carried to the lounge, their huge hands wrapped round her bottom and across her chest. Oh how she hated it, she had tried to let her father know how she felt but he just wouldn't listen. Such a weak man, and oh, how she hated them both.

She grew up despising them, she grew up knowing that one day she would have her revenge and that's what had made life bearable at times. She more or less brought herself up, cooking, cleaning and making sure she was neat and tidy for school. She could remember doing these things from a young age. No one had ever suspected that she looked after herself. After all, her mother and father were members of the local church. Who would ever believe such a thing? And she would never dare speak to anyone outside of the family about how she was feeling. Her mother had seen to that, threatening her with a long cane she kept in the kitchen. She would tap the stick ever so lightly near Clementine making sure she could feel the gust of air going past her face, but not quite touching her. Not to bruise her, oh no, that would never happen. Just a slight tap. But that was enough to frighten Clementine. And of course there was the 'look'. Oh God, she could still remember that look. A hard, cold stare from her mother was enough to frighten any child. And you know, when she thought about it her mother's eyes were empty. Almost as if she had no soul and no heart. Her mother was a very cold and calculating woman, who if she were honest, absolutely hated children.

As told to Clementine on numerous occasions about how she had been a 'mistake'. And oh, how Clementine had paid for that mistake. She would often be called 'ugly' or 'fat' and the comment that hurt the most was 'useless'.

"No one will ever love you. You will never be anything in life," her mother would often tell her. And of course, her father, sitting there, never defending Clementine, he just sat there. She *hated* him with such a passion, probably more than her mother because he did nothing to help her, nothing to save her and absolutely nothing to protect her. But all the while Clementine was plotting, plotting to torture them, plotting to inflict pain and plotting to watch them die. Those are the thoughts that would give her great delight, lift her when she was feeling low and have her almost wet her pants with glee. Oh yes, revenge was indeed sweet. But she had to bide her time, the timing had to be impeccable.

Over the years, Clementine had become a very resilient individual who could never quite see any good in anyone. She had a very unique and cynical view of the world and had a mistrust of everyone around her. She always felt that people had an ulterior motive and were not genuine. She was, she was genuine, there was absolutely nothing wrong with her, it was everyone else!

She could present herself as being very friendly, whilst inside seething with an anger that felt like a physical pain, angry at the world, angry at people and well, just plain angry. And that anger could scare her. On many occasions she would be quite afraid of her thoughts and plans, but had over the years, become accustomed to them. So the 'norm' for her was never quite 'normal'. She didn't want to be normal, she liked being different.

Some years before, she had met a handsome man in the library where she worked. She knew instantly that she liked him. He was very tall and lean and reminded her of herself in a lot of ways. He physically did look like her, and when she spoke to him, she felt as though she had known him for years. She was twenty-three and had never been with a man nor had she ever even been on a date, so when he asked her out for a coffee, she jumped at the chance. She was so excited and felt a stirring in her that she had never felt before. She knew what he felt about her, because remember, Clementine could read people's minds. She knew his inner thoughts and this urged her on, almost as if it were physically pushing her towards him. He had looked at her in a way no other man had and she knew he wanted to make love to her. He found her physically attractive — her! Would you believe it? This was the Clementine that had been told incessantly that she was ugly. She hadn't really thought about it but anytime she saw him it had always been him that had arranged when they were meeting and where. She never met any of his friends and he very rarely spoke about work but that didn't bother Clementine. She just loved being with him, watching him and touching him.

The debonair Ethan worked in finance and had a bachelor pad in the city. He was a very sociable man so it was most surprising that he had fallen for Clementine (if indeed that's what it was). He had many friends and led a privileged and busy life. He loved fast cars, casinos and nightclubs and was a confident individual who had never failed at anything in his whole life. He came from a privileged background and had attended private school right up until his graduation from one of the most renowned universities in the UK. So it was most unusual that he had started to date Clementine. Now, this interlude with Clementine hadn't interfered with his lifestyle in the city and he made sure there was never a chance that the two would ever meet. He saw her as 'his means to an end'. He had a fondness for her, he wasn't quite sure why but he did and he was happy enough using her whenever suited him. He adapted his whole being when he was with Clementine. It wasn't him but someone else. Someone slightly more sedate, someone slightly more thoughtful and someone slightly more loving. He had a huge gambling problem which had begun at university. His profound addiction surfaced when he worked and lived in the city but was very discreetly put away when he visited his home village. He owed thousands of pounds to different casinos throughout London and had managed to evade a beating or even prosecution for some years now. So Ethan in a sense was a 'soul', a man who had lost his way, a man who was, if truth be told, as complicated and messed up as Clementine. Maybe that was the attraction?

Clementine and Ethan dated over the next few months and Clementine knew that she was falling in love with him. Everything was going well and she had seen a side to herself that had shown compassion, patience and love. She had never felt those things before. Oh yes, she was most definitely in love with the man of her dreams. Mr Ethan Clark Robertson. The name just flowed from her mouth and it felt wonderful, just wonderful. They went out for long walks, went for coffee and out for dinner. She felt as though she were floating on air when she was with him. She didn't mind that she always paid for the meal or coffee. She was in love. She had never had the confidence to speak to someone the way she could talk to him, so easy and she always felt so very comfortable in his company. Her mother and father never asked her where she was going. Her mother was too busy playing whore and her father just doing absolutely nothing. *Oh God, he's such an absolute wimp!* thought Clementine. No protective or safe thoughts ever came into that messed up head of hers when she thought of him. So Ethan made her life worth living and made her feel so very special. She knew it was approaching the time where making love was inevitable, and of course, she was apprehensive, scared and yet so very excited.

She had never been with a man before so the more she thought about it, the more she would tremble at the thought! She couldn't wait. Well it wouldn't be too long that she would have to, anyway. Ethan had booked a room at a posh hotel in nearby Wetherhall. "Clementine," he said. "Could you possibly lend me £100? There's a God-awful problem with my bank, God knows what it is but I need to pay the hotel."

"Of course," she said. "No problem." Because it wasn't a problem for her, this was the love of her life, the man she had fallen in love with and the only person on the planet that just 'got her'. She could never refuse him anything. Clementine prepared herself for the night ahead and packed a lovely pink and cream nightie, not very sexy it has to be said but sexy enough for her. She felt quite risqué and naughty when she packed it in her case. Oh my, she exclaimed look at little old me. Getting ready for a really good seeing to. She chuckled at the thought of the night ahead.

And oh my God, she wasn't disappointed. After a lovely meal and drinks they both went to the room. Everything had felt so very natural and right. Ethan made love to her and kissed every part of her body from her head to her toes. He made her feel like the sexiest woman in the world and the actual deed! Well, suffice to say, she saw heaven, NO she REALLY saw heaven! God, it was amazing. It was everything she had dreamed of and more. The next morning she turned over in bed and there he was, facing her in all his glory. She stared at him, so handsome, so gorgeous and he was hers! His long eyelashes resting on the edge of his cheekbones, his strong nose, his full and inviting mouth. *Oh God, I could stare at him all day. He just makes me feel complete,* she thought. He opened his eyes and they both smiled. And at that moment Clementine knew she would never feel like that again. It was sheer perfection. She wanted to capture it, bottle it and keep it forever. They showered and dressed and both went downstairs to have breakfast. She felt as though everyone was staring at her. She laughed quietly and felt an immense sense of pride, look at who she was with. *Isn't he gorgeous,* she thought to herself.

Oddly enough after their wonderful night at the hotel Ethan had become slightly withdrawn and quiet. She did ask him what was wrong but he always had the same reply. "Nothing." And that was it. No other explanation. She had thought everything was just wonderful, she couldn't believe her life could be so complete and she would feel so fulfilled but there was a definite change in Ethan and poor

Clementine couldn't understand why. Ethan, on the other hand, felt very differently. It had been an OK shag, nothing special but, hey whatever made her happy for a while he thought. He had even found it difficult to get an erection, something that would normally be no problem for him. But, needs must. He started to pluck up the courage to ask her if she could loan him some money. He didn't foresee that being a problem, but of course there was the fact that he would still have to see her, and he wasn't sure if he could continue to do that. Even the thought of her touching him made him recoil.

His mind was made up. He would ask her this evening at dinner. He knew he was in deep shit to some of the most hard-nosed money lenders in London so he had to do something. He couldn't go to Mummy because she would then know he wasn't flawless and he simply couldn't bear that. So it had to be Clementine he would ask. That evening he had complimented Clementine on her dress and hair.

"Oh, thank you, Ethan," she said, holding his hand. Ethan felt a sense of revulsion and was almost physically sick but he smiled and kissed her on the lips. Christ! How much more could he take.

"Clementine, my love," he said. "I have something rather important to ask you."

Oh, do you, Ethan, she thought, her heart thumping loudly. "What is it?"

She waited with anticipation for those words, 'will you marry me?' But out came the words, "Could you lend me £10,000?"

She jumped back slightly, pulling her hand from his. "What?" she said. "What did you say?"

"Oh, my love, I am in some trouble in London and I really need £10,000 or they are going to kill me."

"'They', who are 'they'?" she said.

"Oh, just some financiers I got involved with and the deals have fallen through. Please, Clementine, could you help me?"

Clementine had no hesitation in her answer. "Of course, my darling, of course I will help. I will transfer the money this evening." She noticed that things did not feel the same after that. Clementine knew that he was becoming more and more withdrawn. Not touching her, not kissing her and always looking as if he just didn't want to be anywhere near her. Her world was crumbling and he had asked to speak to her that evening about their relationship. Clementine couldn't understand why she couldn't read his mind, she had no idea what was going on. It might be because she was so emotionally involved with him, she wasn't sure? It was odd because that had never happened to her before.

Ethan had suddenly decided that the romance of the century was over, that's right — *over*. "What," she had exclaimed. "What have I done wrong? Please tell me, Ethan, what have I done wrong?"

He couldn't answer her, his head bowed with no excuse as to why their relationship was ending. And there it was, she looked at him and he reminded her so much of her father. Standing there, a pitiful excuse of a man. And all those feelings of hatred and evil came flooding back, almost as if they had never been away.

"Can't we talk about this?" she said. "Please, Ethan, come and meet me in the woods next to my house. *please* Ethan, *please*."

"OK," he said. "I will come."

Ethan felt like a bit of a heel treating her like this but his debts were paid for now, and he had become rather tired of her. "Of course I will come. Around seven? Does that sound OK. We can talk but I have made up my mind, Clementine, you won't talk me round." Ethan knew that this so-called relationship had run its course. She had proved to be of use to him but he was done now. He knew his gambling addiction hadn't gone and he desperately needed to get back to London. *I know where she is if I need her,* he thought. And that was Ethan's take on this. It was as simple as that. He had used and abused her. He didn't care that she loved him. He was a selfish and manipulating man who had got what he wanted. Unfortunately, poor Clementine had paid the price.

But Clementine wasn't as stupid as he had thought. He had totally misjudged her and he had absolutely no idea of what she was capable of. "There is a lovely inlet of water just next to my house," said Clementine.

"OK," he replied. "See you at seven." He waved his hand, walking away from her almost as if he were being dismissive.

What a shit! she thought. *What a complete and utter shit!* Clementine smirked because she knew what she was going to do at seven and talking was the last thing on her evil and wicked mind. She laughed silently, poor Ethan. He had no idea of the night that lay before him and she had no idea of just how far her wickedness would go.

Clementine couldn't eat that night. Her mother, father and her sitting at the table in silence as they did every night. She just couldn't eat a thing, she was so excited about the night that lay ahead. "Are you not eating?" her father said.

"No," she replied. "I just don't feel well. I'm going for a walk." She turned around quickly and flounced out of the door.

As she walked towards the inlet of water, she saw Ethan standing there, kicking the twigs on the ground and looking rather awkward. Oh, how she despised him now. She couldn't believe how her complete and utter love for him had turned into sheer hatred. But hey, it would be OK. She wasn't that bothered about what she had planned for him. In fact, she was rather looking forward to it. "Hi, Ethan," she shouted.

He turned round with a slight smile looking so bloody gorgeous! "How are you?" he said.

"Oh, I'm OK. Listen, would you mind if we go somewhere really private?"

"Eh, well, OK," he replied.

She knew he didn't really feel comfortable being with her but probably felt he had to go, just so he looked as if he were half human and had some feelings. They walked together towards her very private and wonderful hideaway. As they both went inside she could see by the look on his face that he wasn't expecting to see what he did.

"Oh my God!! This is amazing, Clementine." There were candles everywhere, glowing warmly in corners of the room, a small but rather tattered couch with some cushions on it and the loveliest smell of lavender drifted above his head. "This is heaven," he said. "Does no one know this exists?"

"No," she said. "No one." Ethan turned around quite

sharply because the tone in her voice had changed somewhat. When he looked at her he was rather stunned because there in front of him was a very changed person. No longer the gentle and subtle look of a woman he thought he knew but that of a menacing and dark woman.

Who the hell was this? he thought.

"Now, now, Ethan. Don't be afraid. It's me, your Clementine."

Oh, no, he thought to himself. *It so is not.* He had become rooted to where he was standing and began to fear what lay ahead for him. He knew then that he was in trouble and he was *never* getting out of that hideaway again.

"Ethan, are you scared?" she croaked. "Really? Scared of, boring and gentle me?"

"No," he said. "Of course not."

"OK then," she said rather sheepishly. "Come with me and sit down, let's have our cosy chat."

He reluctantly began to sit down when *whack*! A loud thump hit the back of his head. The pain was excruciating and he fell on to the couch holding the bloody wound. His fingers touched the back of his head and they were covered in blood. He could barely see Clementine, everything was a blur and then nothing, just black. When he woke he was chained to a post in the middle of the room, he looked down and he was naked. *What the Fuck,* he thought. His head ached and he couldn't keep his eyes open. He drifted in and out of consciousness for what seemed like a lifetime. There was no sign of Clementine. He was all alone, no noises to be heard but the sound of his own breathing fast and heavy. No candles, no longer the lovely smell of lavender, just the smell of his own blood and urine. Little did he know, but he had become Clementine's first victim.

Meanwhile Clementine had skipped back to the house feeling joyful and happy. "God, that felt good," she said. "I'm' such a bad girl."

"Who's that downstairs?" bellowed her mother.

"Oh, just me," she said. "Just getting some hot chocolate and then off to bed." Clementine slept like a baby that night and faced the next day feeling fulfilled and content. God this was so exciting, what would she do next? He was her plaything, her puppet and she could do with him what she wanted and no one would ever know. "Oh," she sniggered. "I am such a naughty girl." Oh my god, the possibilities were endless. She knew that he was absolutely terrified, she felt it, remember she knew what he was thinking. She didn't return to her hideaway for a few days, she couldn't quite remember when she had left him. Well, all days were the same, how was she supposed to know?

Off she popped to the hideaway, she had packed a small picnic for her and Ethan, still hoping that maybe, just maybe there was a chance he would change his mind and love her again. As she entered the hideaway she could smell the most foul of smells. *What the hell was that*? she thought. She walked in and there he was. Poor Ethan, covered in vomit, shit and urine. Dried blood on his face and pleading, "Please, Clementine, please help me. Please." Tears were streaming down his face. His voice was weak and pathetic.

"Oh, do shut up, Ethan, you sound like an absolute wimp! Well let me tell you, you are certainly not getting any of *my* picnic. I will eat alone and *outside*!"

"Clementine, *please*.

Clementine could barely hear him. She quietly closed the door behind her and carefully put some tree branches against the door. *There,* she thought. *He's safe in there.*

Ethan soon realised she wasn't coming back, he was going to die. There was no one to hear him and no one to help him. He began to pray. "Please, Lord, please help me, Oh Lo…" He never finished his sentence. A black eeriness descended upon the hideaway, encompassing the horror that lay inside.

Clementine sat under a tree in the sunshine eating her sandwiches. She listened to the birds in the trees and had a short nap before heading back home. She wasn't going back into the hideaway, not while he was still there stinking the place out! No chance. Clementine began to randomly dance, the sun on her face and her bare feet on the grass. *This is just bliss* she sang to herself. Clementine thought for a minute. *Right, I can't and won't think of him again. I'm better than that smelly, dirty, vile person.* And that's exactly what she did. She completely forgot all about him. Although, she was sure there were some nights she could hear his screams coming from deep in the woods. She wasn't quite sure though and it never really interrupted her sleep, so… what the hell? He was a rat so it made sense that he live like a rat and die like one.

A few months later, Clementine was walking in the village, swinging her bag and humming a tune to herself when a small, rather obese lady stopped her.

"Hello, Clementine," she said. "Do you remember me?"

"Sorry, no. Who are you?"

"I'm Ethan's great aunt, Dorothy. Don't you remember,

you came to my house a short while ago for afternoon tea."

"Oh, yes," Clementine shrieked. "I remember you now!"

"How are you, dear," she said with a rather cynical tone to her voice.

"I'm OK, and how are you?"

"Well, my dear, not so good if I'm to be brutally honest. I know you had told everyone in the village that Ethan had, how can we put it, *dumped you*! His mother and I were rather shocked at that I can tell you, but there you go that's men for you. He always could be rather fickle."

"Oh, I would never have said Ethan was fickle," Clementine exclaimed. "Rather focussed and organised I thought!"

"Well, that was probably the private school education," she said, rather proudly.

"Was it?" said Clementine. "I went to the village school, we weren't that privileged, I'm afraid."

"Ethan was sent away from the age of four, to a private school in France," she said.

"France!" exclaimed Clementine. "Why France?"

"Well, my dear, that was the best private school at the time and his mother always wanted the very best for him. I've got to be honest, Clementine, we were rather surprised when we heard he had started dating you."

"Oh, thanks," said Clementine.

"Oh no, dear, I don't mean it like that, I just mean, ahh, well I don't know what I mean. Sorry if I've offended you, I sometimes just open my mouth and don't think about what I'm saying. Sorry dear.

"Anyway," she said, sounding rather embarrassed, "his

mother is beside herself with worry. You know, he hasn't written or telephoned in over six months. I mean, what is he thinking of, worrying his dear old mum like that."

"Well, I really don't know what's happened," stammered Clementine, slightly trembling at the lie she was telling.

"Oh, Clementine, I'm sorry, I'm upsetting you. I know you loved him dearly. I'm so sorry. Do you have time for a cup of tea?"

"Ahh, no," she said. "Thank you, anyway, but I'm rather busy today."

"Oh, that's fine, don't worry, we could maybe organise tea one day, dear? Maybe with myself and Ethan's mum? What do you think, would you be OK with that?"

"Yes, yes, of course," she said as she walked away rather hurriedly.

"Of course. I will be in contact. Lovely to see you," she shouted at Clementine.

"Yeah, ahh, the same. Bye."

Oh shit, thought Clementine, *Shit, shit, shit. What am I going to do. I mean I've done nothing wrong here. Shit!* Clementine knew that Great Aunt Dorothy was thinking something bad had happened to Ethan, remember she can read people's minds. *What am I going to do?* After some thought, Clementine knew exactly what to do. A few days later she rang Great Aunt Dorothy. "How about a picnic in the woods for our day out?"

"Oh, my dear," she said. "That sounds rather lovely. I will let my sister, Emilia, know.

"Is the 10th July OK?" she said. "It's a Saturday. I'm happy to prepare the picnic, and we can eat in the most idyllic place in the world."

"Where's that?" she said.

"Oh you probably won't know it, it's just off from the woodland walk. I go there quite often, its rather beautiful."

"Oh, that sounds lovely, Clementine. Thank you."

See you on the 10th at one p.m., just at the entrance gate to the woodland walk.

Clementine put the phone down, her heart beating fast and loud, as if it were going to jump out her chest. She rubbed her hands together. "Oh I'm so clever, so very clever, it's scary." She laughed. She knew Great Aunt Dorothy lived on her own, and so did Ethan's mum. What else could she think or do? The opportunity had been handed to her on a plate and she just had to seize it. She caught sight of her reflection in the mirror. "Oh, dear God, who's that looking back at me? It's not plain, old, boring Clementine," she sneered. Oh no, the person looking back at her had narrow, menacing eyes, tight thin lips and seethed evil. She loved seeing herself like that. That was the true her

Saturday 10th July came. Clementine made a glorious picnic. All the usual nibbles but with an added touch. Just a sprinkling of Valium. Powdered and in the salmon sandwiches and some in the ham as well. Just in case they don't like salmon she laughed. She sniggered to herself because she had thought of everything. She knew that the area would be busy, especially on a beautiful Saturday but she wasn't going to the usual places in the woods, she had an extensive knowledge of the trees and greenery and knew of a trail that would take them deep into the woods where no one would find them.

"Hi, ladies," she screamed excitedly. "How are we both today?"

"Oh, we are fine, Clementine," said Great Aunt Dorothy. Ethan's mum just smiled, and said a quiet, "Hello." She looked as though there was a nasty smell under her nose, you know, the type that think they are better than everyone else.

"Well, I've brought our picnic as I promised, are you both ready for this gorgeous walk?"

"Oh yes," they both said. "We are. Thank you, Clementine," they said in unison.

"No problem," she remarked. "Let's go. We can chat along the way."

The ladies' pace of walking was very slow so Clementine had to be a bit more patient than usual. Patience was not one of her strengths. She normally wouldn't be spending any of her precious time with these 'oldies' but then needs must. As they were walking they started chatting about Ethan.

"I find this all very worrying and odd," his mother said. "He's missed my birthday, and he has never done that before. I'm thinking of going to the police. What do you think, Clementine?"

"Oh, well, I can't say," she said. "That's your decision, not mine. He's a grown man, and you know he could be quite selfish at times, so maybe it's just that part of him that's rearing its ugly head."

Ethan's mum looked at her with disgust. "Selfish! My Ethan? Never! I've never known him to be such a way. I don't know who you were courting, Clementine, but that doesn't sound like my boy. Not at all." Her voice was loud and angry.

"Oh, I'm so sorry," said Clementine. "I didn't mean to upset you, please accept my apologies."

"Very well," she replied curtly. "Let's say no more about it. I should probably have contacted the police before now, but I thought he would walk through the door. This behaviour is most unlike him. I'm definitely contacting the police on Monday morning."

"What about Ethan's work?" said Clementine. "Have you spoken to anyone there?"

Oh, he had resigned because he had some stupid idea he wanted to travel around the world. Did he say that to you, Clementine?"

"Well, now that you come to mention it, he did say something about that, but we were splitting up so I didn't give it any more thought. Sorry," said Clementine looking as if butter wouldn't melt. She suddenly had a flashback to the letter she had typewritten to Ethan's place of work, explaining that he was off around the world. She had totally forgotten all about that! She was indeed so very clever!

After a few hours, the ladies were becoming tired. There was no longer a path to walk on, and although it was only 2.45 in the afternoon, it was getting quite dark in the woods. "Could we sit and have our picnic now?" they both said.

"Of course," said Clementine. "Sorry, I'm forgetting the two of you are rather frail and old," she said sniggering.

"*WHAT*!!" Great Aunt Dorothy replied. "Not us, Clementine. We are as fit as fleas."

"Sorry again, I rather seem to be saying the wrong things. Let's sit and eat," she said rather sheepishly. All three sat on the grass. Clementine laid down a beautiful picnic cover and put out her delicious picnic. "Please, try my sandwiches. Salmon or ham?" She waited with bated breath as both took from the plate and started to eat.

"Oh, these are delicious," both exclaimed.

"Please try some of my elderberry and gooseberry cordial (*with an added twist, of course,* she thought). I make this myself."

"Lovely, Clementine, that's delicious. What a lovely picnic. And what a view here. We have both been on the woodland walk, but never came as far as this."

"I know, it's lovely isn't it," said Clementine.

"Are you not eating, Clementine?" they asked.

"No. I'm afraid I have a bit of an upset tummy. I will just have a few crackers. Please have another sandwich, there're plenty."

"Oh they are delicious," they both replied. "We certainly will." The three of them laughed. "I think I might have a nap," said Great Aunt Dorothy. I'm suddenly feeling rather sleepy. You don't mind do you, Clementine?"

"No, not at all. I think I will have a rest as well." Soon both ladies were fast asleep. Great Aunt Dorothy had leaned against a magnificent oak tree and then very gently 'slumped' down on to the grass. Ethan's mother lay against a rather large stone and very quickly drifted off to sleep, dropping her glass of juice in the process. She looked so serene when she slept. Not the cow that she really was, not the cow who had dared to upset Clementine. She lifted the picnic from the ground and packed all the things away. Clementine started to walk away, rather slowly almost at a snail's pace, so she could glance back and see the both of them looking peaceful and content under the glare of the sun, shaded by the trees. Oh look how perfect this all looks. The two of them lying there in the most beautiful place on earth. Clementine knew she had given them enough Valium to render them helpless so she wasn't worried that they would awaken any time soon. "Do enjoy your rest, ladies," she quietly said, as she was walking away. Clementine smiled a rather demure smile.

She was at work a few days later when one of her regular customers in the library said to her, "Clementine, have you heard about Emelia Robertson?"

"No," she said. "Who's she? Who's she?"

"She's Ethan's mum, you know the chap you used to go out with."

"Oh, right, I didn't really know her. Why, what's happened? Well, she's just disappeared, no one knows what's happened, she lives in that big house just outside the village. It only came to light because her dog could be heard barking. People who were walking past had reported it to the police, and they've been to her house but there's no sign of her. The poor dog was starving, they say its lucky to be alive. Everyone's talking about it. She loved that dog. Someone said they had saw you with her last Saturday? At the woodland walk."

"Oh, yes," said Clementine. "I saw her then. She was going for a walk with Ethan's Great Aunt Dorothy, but I didn't go with them. Should I speak to the police do you think?"

"Well, I would," he said.

What did he mean? Did he think she had something to hide? Stupid man! He had his own secrets, as Clementine knew only too well.

She contacted the police straight away, explaining that she had seen the two ladies at the entrance to the woodland walk. "Were they heading in there do you think?" asked PC Nicholls.

"No, I think they said they were going up to Primrose Point."

"Really? I'm quite surprised at that. That's a bit of a distance, and they are elderly women. Are you sure?"

"Yes, definitely, that's what they said."

"So, we had thought she was on her own, you say someone else was with her?"

Clementine hesitated slightly. "Yes, eh Dorothy Parker, she's a relative I think."

"Well, thank you," he said. "I will let the DCI know. It's a bit of a mystery that both of them go missing at the same time. They've probably got lost in the woods."

"It sure sounds like that," said Clementine. "I do hope you find them."

The local police had searched the woodland walk, but they had only searched the actual public walk and not the one that she knew of, the one that trails off deep into the woods. There is no path evident to the human eye, but Clementine knew of a path that was well hidden and they didn't. She laughed as she thought of the sheer incompetence of the police. They hadn't searched any further because they were idiots, mere idiots. The walk that Clementine had taken them on was 'off the beaten track'. No one knew those woods like her, absolutely no one. She knew it would be a very, very, long time before, and if, those ladies were ever found. She sighed, smirked and then started to laugh uncontrollably. She felt euphoric, amazingly intelligent and far superior to anyone who deemed to enter her world.

Clementine hadn't been very well since the unfortunate episode with Ethan. Always nauseous, tired and just feeling absolutely rotten. She had noticed she was getting a bit of a 'tummy' but thought no more about it. She had started to feel movement in her stomach but had absolutely no idea what it was. She had no one she could talk to about it so she had just kept her thoughts to herself, well she was used to doing that. Then one night she was in bed when she felt a searing pain shoot through her full body. *What the hell is this!!* she thought. She was scared and in agony but couldn't and wouldn't cry out to her mother and father for help. She fell from her bed onto the floor and was on all fours when she felt a tremendous need to 'push'. Sweat was dripping from her face and she couldn't stop herself from feeling the urge to get whatever it was out! She screamed into her pillow, grabbing it with both hands on the floor, her knuckles white with the hold. One push, two pushes and then on the third push she felt something thud onto the floor. She slowly looked round and there lying on the floor covered in blood was a *baby*! *Yuk,* she thought, *why the hell was that thing in my body?* She could see the cord still attached to the 'thing' and pushed one more time and a blubber of jelly just plopped onto the carpet. Clementine ran into the toilet and began to clean herself. She felt the grotesque, sticky, smelly blood all over her legs and even down below! She gave absolutely no thought or regard to the human life lying on the floor in her bedroom. She slowly walked back in to her normally neat and clean bedroom to be met with blood and gunge on the floor, and of course, that thing was still there. *Right,* she thought, *What to do?? What to do??* She paced for a few minutes and before she could think any further 'the thing' started to make a noise. Oh God, I need to get this out of the house or they will hear and come to my bedroom. She quickly wrapped it up in an old sheet and quietly walked downstairs. She stood at the bottom of the stairs for a few seconds, almost as if she were having second thoughts about what she was going to do, and then began to walk again with no clear thought of what she was going to do next. She found herself walking through the woods, and although it was pitch black, she wasn't afraid. Remember these were her woods, she had always felt safe and happy here. Her first and most important thought was where she was putting this thing so no one would know. She soon found herself standing outside her hideaway. *I know exactly where to put it she thought.* She walked a few more steps to the water and placed some small rocks inside the sheet. She wrapped it up very tightly and placed it gently in the water, watching it sink almost immediately to the bottom. Clementine stood for a few seconds and decided to pray. "Oh Lord, please look after me and make sure I'm ok. I know I can be bad, but as you've just seen, Lord, it's not always my fault. Take care of me. Please, Lord. Take care of me." Not a solitary thought or prayer for the human life she had just discarded and absolutely no regard for the disgusting deed she had just carried out. None at all. She slowly walked back to the house, quietly cleared up the mess and then simply went to bed, sleeping as soundly as she had ever done.

Life moved on for Clementine and very soon Ethan, the two old ladies and the 'thing' became a distant and forgotten part of her life. Her daily life was always challenging with her mother trying her best to shag every male within a thirty mile radius of the village and her father struggling every day just to rise from his bed and do anything. Such a 'slouch', such a 'waste of human life', well both of them were to be honest. But Clementine never let the two of them intrude on her life, she was highly admired in the village but she knew that people thought she was 'dim', 'boring' and well if truth be told, probably a bit 'thick'. People spoke about her while she was in listening distance. She wasn't that bothered, she didn't care, she could put on a 'face'. You know, the kind of face everyone feels so sorry for. Outside a boring, sad lady who had never married and had no life, but inside a lady with secrets and an ego that would rock their effing worlds. "Fools!" she exclaimed. "Utter and complete fools."

The years passed and Clementine was looking forward to celebrating her fiftieth birthday. Her thoughts went back to when she had first met Ethan and how she fell instantly in love with this gorgeous man. I *wonder how long it's been since I saw Ethan? I know,* she thought, *I will take a picnic and some champagne to the hideaway. I know he would want to celebrate my birthday. He's bound to still be there and well, he's maybe changed his mind about dumping me. Yes,* she thought excitedly. *I will do just that,* talking as if it were yesterday and not all those years ago, twenty-seven, to be precise.

On the morning of her birthday her father had tried to make breakfast 'somewhat special'.

"Get up, Clementine," her father said.

Clementine woke abruptly thinking, who the hell is that? Her father *never* did that, *never*. And yet, there he was shouting at her to get up.

"It's your birthday, you're fifty today!" He sounded rather excited.

Oh, my God. Listen to him. I can't believe it. Clementine rose from her bed and went downstairs, where a beautiful breakfast spread was laid out for her. And there he was, sitting at the top of the table, looking, would you believe, rather proud. Clementine couldn't believe it. "Thank you, Father," she said. "Thank you so much. This looks lovely."

"Sit down and eat," he said. "I've made you a card as well."

Clementine looked into the eyes of someone she barely knew, someone she had hated for years, who the hell was this man? A lost and sad soul, just like her, and for the first time in her life, Clementine felt sorry for him. She leaned over and gave him a very gentle hug. He lifted one hand to her back, patting her gently but rather awkwardly. It wasn't until that moment that Clementine realised he was just a frail old man. When she had hugged his shoulders all she could feel were bone. When she had looked into his eyes and seen his face (almost for the first time) he looked old, tired and sad. "Thank you, Father, this is lovely."

Clementine had just sat down when there was a loud noise. 'Bang!' The door was thrown open and there stood a dishevelled drunk woman. "Morning all," her mother said.

"What's happening here?"

"It's my birthday, Mother, as well you know and Father has made a lovely breakfast for us all to sit and enjoy."

"Mmmmm, really! No ta," she exclaimed. "I'm off to bed, I'm knackered." She looked at Clementine and then looked at Clementine's father and sniggered. She sniggered! How dare she! All the good feelings that Clementine had felt, the compassion, the love and the empathy for her father were wiped out in an instant. And do you know why. He just sat there and said nothing, absolutely nothing.

And Clementine felt as though she were back to being five years old again. All those feelings of worthlessness, shame and neglect came flooding back. *She needs to go,* thought Clementine, *she needs to go. I've no idea when or how but she needs to go. Hell I think would be the best place for her, yes Hell. That's where I will send her. It's been a long time coming.*

Clementine wanted to enjoy her birthday, so as planned she got herself washed and dressed and headed down to her hideaway. She was trying to remember the last time she was there but her head had become so scrambled she honestly couldn't remember. *Oh, I do hope Ethan is still there,* she thought. *I've got the champers and glasses. It would be great if he could help me celebrate my birthday.* As she approached the hideaway she started to get flashes in her head, flashes of Ethan being chained to the wooden post, flashes of him screaming and asking for help, memories of the smells. Oh god, what had happened to Ethan, had someone hurt him? She approached the hideaway with some caution (almost as if she had never been there). She slowly walked in and the smell was absolutely awful. There was no sign of Ethan but what she did see were empty handcuffs next to a wooden beam with men's clothes strewn all over the floor and what she thought were bits of bone all around the hideaway. *I wonder what's happened here,* she thought, *that's odd. It's probably been foxes or badgers. There was no sign of Ethan. He must have gone,* she thought. *Just upped and left. Typical him!* She began to clear the bones and debris from the hideaway. She made a fire and burnt the clothes and then threw the handcuffs in the nearby lake. It wasn't long before it was looking neat and tidy again. I've neglected this place she said. And then she slowly thought, *I don't think I've been back here for a long time. I get pains in my head with all the confusion and I get so very tired.* She smiled. Yes, that's it. I know what's happened now. Time has just passed so very quickly. *Well, all fine now,* she thought to herself. *Everything neat and tidy, just how I like it.*

Clementine was back at work the next day but her mind was pre-occupied with thoughts of wondering how she was going to get rid of her mother, you know the pain in the arse, the thorn in her side, the whore, the absolute and utter waste of life.

If truth be told Clementine didn't really know her mother, she knew of the cruelty and disregard for her father and her and she knew of her mother's philandering ways but as for her as a person? No, she knew nothing about her. Her father had told her that her mother (Rosina) had been brought up, or shall we say dragged up, in a tenement flat in Manchester. Her memories of Rosina's own mother were those that involved her being beaten on a daily basis by her alcoholic husband so no surprises that Rosina was 'her father's child'. She didn't know how to love or care for another human being. They lived in a poverty-stricken area in Manchester and her younger brother had died when he was three. TB? She couldn't quite remember but that's what she thought it was. She had heard it being spoken about by her mother and father and how her brother was always 'chesty'. She could never remember a time when her brother was well. He always looked so ill. She was four when he was born but she could clearly remember him and the painful memories when he died. Her mother, the poor soul, was never the same after he died. It was her who had carried the coffin, a small wooden box with a single flower on top. Her father had been too bereft to carry out the dreadful deed so her mother had to do it, as if that were her duty. After he died she had no spark, there was no laughter in the house and she very rarely saw her mum smile. She could clearly remember she never saw her mum without bruising somewhere on her skinny pale arms or her prematurely old face. Always tired and always sad. Rosina remembered her mother being beaten by her father, she was there, she saw everything. He didn't hide the beatings, I mean he would always say she deserved them. Almost as if she were 'asking for it'. She had no memory of hugs or kisses or being told she was loved. She had no regard for herself never mind anyone else. And she did kind of love Clementine in her own rather odd way. Rosina felt she did the best she could with her daughter. I mean, she didn't want any children, it was her husband who goaded her into becoming pregnant. She never felt any 'bond' between her and Clementine and had left the feeding and changing to her husband so there was never any physical or emotional contact between mother and baby. Back in the day there was no support available for her, not that she wanted or needed it but there was no one to make sure she was coping OK. No one. She was an only child just like Clementine. She had no friends or family so she was just left to get on with it.

When she had met Clementine's father, Frank, he had fallen in love with her straight away, the same could not be said for her falling in love with him. He was kind and showed her generosity that she had never seen before so when he asked her to get married she jumped at the chance of some kind of a better life. She soon became very bored with her 'better life' and opted for the opportunity to jump on a train into London and meet new friends, mostly male she would admit but people who showed her attention and gave her the time of day. Over the years she had built up quite a crowd of males who she knew would keep her entertained and she didn't ever see any problem with bringing them home for a few drinks. What about the sex? It meant absolutely nothing to her so her thoughts about it were rather different from everyone else's. It was a physical thing, a need to do thing, it wasn't about love. My God! She had never loved anyone. She didn't know what love was for heaven's sake. The nearest she had come to love, was the feelings she had for her husband which were more of a friendship rather than love. She did respect him, though others around her would tell her incessantly that she didn't, but she knew that she did. So when she brought her male friends home she honestly thought it was a nice thing to do, not humiliating for Clementine, and certainly not humiliating for her husband. She did try and be a nice person but everyone else around her didn't see the true her. Well, that's what she felt. What a pity that Clementine, her one and only daughter, despised her so much, and her husband was disgusted by her behaviour. But do you know. that would never stop her living the life that she felt comfortable with. Never. No one would do that. Sadly her life would be cut much shorter than she would ever dream of.

Clementine's mother's health had deteriorated over the years so she should be easy to get rid of. But how? Her mother had a medicine cabinet full of medication, tablets for her heart, liver, kidneys and blood pressure. *Mmmm,* she thought, *I could research what the side effects of these medicines are and that way no one would ever suspect anything. I could say I'm doing some homework for someone else. Brilliant idea* she thought.

Clementine started her research, looking into side effects and different symptoms associated with all those medications. *Oh, this is too much hard work,* she thought, *I've not got time for this. A pure and simple overdose would suffice, thank you very much.* But how would she get her mother to take an overdose of her heart medication? *Crushed and into her drink* she thought? *How easy is this!* Clementines mother was a well-known patient at the local GP surgery and had become a frequent visitor over the past few years as her health had started to decline. Clementine began to sneak small sentences into conversations with the villagers. Conversations like, "My mother is really struggling with her health you know" or "My mother's social life is disappearing now due to her ill health, it must be hard for her."

And of course the majority of the villagers loved a good old gossip. They would listen to rumour and soak it up like a big wet sponge. Clementine wasted no time in sneaking some of her mother's heart medication out of the cabinet. She opened the capsules and poured the powder into a big mug of hot chocolate. She then lovingly placed pretty pink and white mallows on the top. *Looks delicious,* she thought. She knew the amount to use that would undoubtedly kill her. Quickly and silently, she didn't want her to suffer, she was her mother after all. She carried the hot chocolate upstairs. "Mother, look what I have made you."

"Oh, thank you, Clementine. That's not like you."

"Oh," she said. "I saw you were really tired today, Mother. Now drink it while it's hot. I've even put mallows on top."

Clementines mother drank the hot chocolate. "That was lovely, Clementine, thank you."

"Now lie and rest, Mother, lie and rest." Clementine sneered as she walked out of the room but as she began to walk down stairs she felt a pang of guilt. *What the hell have I done*, she thought, feeling dreadfully sorry for herself, but then immediately thought, *To hell with her. The bitch deserves all she gets. She will answer to her maker for all her wrongdoings over the years.*

Her mother and father had separate rooms, the sleeping arrangements had been like that for years so he would be none the wiser if she were to feel unwell during the night. Clementine went to bed and was soon drifting off to sleep. Her alarm rang at 6.30 a.m. *Time to get up,* she thought. She went downstairs and began making breakfast. Her father

43

came down a few minutes later.

"Is your mother not up yet?" he said.

"No, not yet," she replied. Clementine and her father sat and ate breakfast, no one spoke. *Nothing new there*, she thought. Clementine got washed and dressed and began to prepare to go to work.

"Rosina!" her father yelled. "It's nearly nine o'clock, time to get up. Rosina!" He left it a few minutes and then went upstairs. He chapped lightly on her door. "Rosina, Rosina," he said quietly. "Are you awake?" He slowly opened the door. He could see the back of her as she was on her side facing the bedroom window. He approached the bed with slight trepidation because he had a horrible feeling that something just wasn't right. He hesitantly looked at her and could clearly see she was dead. "Clementine! Clementine! Oh my God! Clementine!"

Clementine ran upstairs. "What's wrong?"

"Your mother, it's your mother. Oh my God, it's your mother. She's *dead*!"

Clementine looked at her mother and started to cry. "Mummy," she cried. "Mummy, wake up, please wake up." Clementine was bereft, her father was in shock and all that could be heard coming from the bedroom were tears and screams.

Her father telephoned for the doctor, explaining that he had just found his wife dead in bed. Dr Carter came out to the house within minutes of the call. He could see Clementine and her father were both very distressed and escorted them both out of the room. He examined Rosina and pronounced her dead. Dr Carter knew that Rosina had suffered from a serious heart condition for a number of years now and she had been advised to stay off the booze and cigarettes. Rosina never heeded his warning so this was no great surprise that she had died. No surprise at all. He came downstairs and sat with Clementine and her father.

"I'm so very sorry, is there anything I can help you with? Please just ask, it's no bother."

"Could you ask Tom Galloway, the undertaker, to come and get her?" said Clementine's dad.

"Of course," he said. "Do you want to go up and sit with her while I phone?"

"Yes," said Clementine. "Come on, Father, we will sit with her until Mr Galloway comes. I don't understand what has happened, she must have had a heart attack or something, don't you think father?" He didn't answer, her father was a broken man, his hands buried in his head and bowed. The next few days were a complete blur.

It was the day before the funeral and Clementine's father had asked that his wife be brought to the house to spend her last night there. The coffin sat in the middle of the lounge, surrounded by dull and drab furniture and rather dated wallpaper. Clementine wanted some time with her mother on her own.

"Is it OK if I sit with mother for a while?"

"Of course," he said.

Clementine sat at the side of the coffin, the lid sitting halfway up so her mother's head and shoulders could be seen. And would you believe her mother was lying there with a white shroud on. "You have got to be joking." Laughed Clementine. "White and my mother just don't go." Clementine had a small kitchen knife in her pocket and smiled as she slowly brought it out, the silver knife

45

gleaming in front of her. *Now, what am I going to do with you,* she thought. She untied the collar of the shroud and very carefully parted the material so her mother's chest could be seen. And very, very slowly Clementine began to carve a message on her mother's chest. She could feel the pressure of cutting the knife into her mother's dead skin, taking her time as she completed the message. She then stood back and looked at her artwork with pride. 'FUCK YOU' was carved across her mother's bare chest. "There, Mother, what do you think of that?" She then delicately kissed her mother's forehead, carefully tied the shroud and shouted her father back into the lounge. "Thank you, Father, I have said all the things I wanted to say." Clementine began to quietly cry.

"Oh, Clementine, are you all right?" Her father gave her a delicate hug.

"Yes, I'll be fine."

"I worry about you, Clementine, you always keep things bottled up, I never know what you're thinking."

"It's OK, Father," she replied quietly. "I'm fine. Go and sit with Mother. As she left the lounge and was way out of her father's sight, Clementine roughly wiped the tears from her eyes and grinned. *Job done!* she thought. *I feel so much better now.* She smiled a crooked and evil smile.

The day of the funeral arrived. Clementine had been very worried about her father, he was a shell of a man, very frail and just so heartbroken. She knew he couldn't live without Rosina. She may not have to do anything to her father as the impact of losing his beloved Rosina would do it for her.

A few weeks passed and Clementine's father was

becoming more and more depressed. He had closed down not just emotionally but physically. He wasn't eating or sleeping and Clementine had tried to help as much as she could. "Father," she said. "Why don't we sit and have a chat. We could chat about Mother if you would like. Would you like that?"

"Yes, maybe," he said.

"Right, let's do that. How did you and mother meet?"

Clementines father lifted his head. "Oh that was a very long time ago now. Fifty years or more. I had to go to Manchester for some training through work and met her in a pub in the city centre."

"Where did you work, Father?"

"I worked in an iron works in Leeds. I've got to say, Clementine, when I saw your mother, I fell in love with her, instantly. I knew right away that she was the woman for me. We chatted in the pub that day and after that were never really apart. We were married within three months, and she was pregnant within the year. I've not had an unhappy day with her he said. Not one.

Clementine looked at him, her eyes wide with alarm. "Father, have you forgotten all the men she brought back to the house, all the times she came home drunk? Do you not remember?"

Her father looked at her in disgust. "Yes, I do remember those times, but she was my wife and I loved her, Clementine, and I would appreciate that you never bad mouth her again, especially in front of me. *Do you hear me!* His voice was raised and angry.

Clementine had never heard her father raise his voice in anger. She looked at him and thought to herself *Oh my god, he is a complete and utter wimp, he has his head so far up his own arse he can't see straight.* "You know, Father, you are such a disappointment to me," she said.

He bowed his head, not in shame but simply because he couldn't face the truth. It was clear he was a weak man and no one would ever be able to help him. Clementine left the room feeling despondent. Who cares that he's not eating, I certainly don't. I won't be looking after him anymore. He can rot in hell just like his stupid pathetic whore of a wife.

She left the house, slamming the door and cussing about the whole sorry situation. This just fuelled Clementine's thoughts that you can trust no one. People let you down at every turn she shouted. Effing human race! I hate them all! And there it was, the overwhelming emotional surge of pure hatred for mankind and another walk along the pathway to hell. She didn't have a good day at work, she had no time for stupid pathetic people. She did her work but spoke very little to anyone who came into the library. Clementine returned home from work that evening tired and angry. *If he tries to talk to me I will just ignore him*, she thought. He was sitting in his usual chair just staring into space, this pathetic weak man who filled her very soul with such an all-consuming rage. Clementine walked into the kitchen and began preparing her meal, her head reeling with how she was going to get rid of the worthless piece of shit. It would be so easy, he had given up on life, and anyway, what difference did it make that she helped push him towards meeting his maker. She would be doing him a favour, wouldn't she? She owed him NOTHING.

"Clementine," he said weakly. "I don't want anything

to eat, I just want to be left in peace, I want to be left with my own thoughts so please don't force me to do anything I don't want to."

"Of course not, Father," she replied quietly. "If that's what you want, I will do just that. I will respect your wishes." She looked up to the heavens with a large smile on her face and rubbed her hands with an excitement that almost made her pee her pants. Stupid old fool!

Over the next few weeks, Clementine saw her father's health deteriorate right in front of her eyes. It was a wondrous sight to see! She didn't offer him any food or drink, well he wasn't that keen on eating or drinking anyway, so she simply stood back and watched him slowly die.

And then, one day out of the blue there was a knock at the door. *I wonder who that can be,* she thought, *no one ever comes here.* She opened the door and there standing in front of her was a small, well-dressed woman. "Can I help you?" she asked.

"Who are you?" the stranger said.

"I'm Clementine. If you don't mind," she replied. "And this is my house. Now who the hell are you?"

"I'm Grace, your mother's sister, and your aunt. I've been living in New Zealand, and have just come back to this country. I couldn't believe it when I heard about your mother. Sadly we hadn't spoken for years because of a huge rift in the family. I've just been told by someone who knew my family that she had recently died. She also told me where you and your father live. Is he here?"

Clementine was just about to answer when her father

said, "Who's there, Clementine?"

"Ehm it's Mother's sister, Grace. She's just found out about her so she's come to see us. Will I let her in?"

"Of course," he said.

Grace walked in, her strong cheap perfume lingering in the air as she walked past Clementine. Clementine looked at her aunt and she was the living image of her mother. She stepped back slightly.

"Are you all right, dear," she said? "You look as if you've seen a ghost."

"You're very like my mother," she said. "Very like her." Clementine took her coat and showed her into the lounge. "Father, this is Grace, Mother's sister."

Her father struggled to get up from his chair but all of a sudden there was a newfound strength that came from within him. He rose from his chair with a new surge of life and his eyes lit up as if someone had switched a light on behind his eyes. "Good evening, Grace, my name is Frank." He held out one hand and took her hand with the other.

"Oh hello," she said.

"I can't believe how much you look like my Rosina," he muttered.

"Ah yes, well we were twins, you know."

"Oh my God! I had no idea, Rosina never mentioned you. In fact she never spoke of her family. Does she have any more brothers or sisters?"

"No," she replied. "Just me, plain old me."

"Oh no, you're anything but plain," he replied. "Please, Grace, will you stay for dinner?"

"Oh yes, thank you, that would be lovely."

"Where are you staying? You must stay with us, it's no

bother."

"Well, that would be lovely, thank you. I'm in a bed and breakfast in the village, but if the offer is there, I would be more than happy to stay here."

"Of course," he said. "It would be our pleasure wouldn't it, Clementine?"

Clementine stood in the corner of the living room with her mouth wide open and her eyes bulging as if they were on stocks. *What the hell had just happened? Not five minutes ago he was all but dead, and now... Look at him staring at her like some lovesick teenager. Oh God!* She thought, *What the hell next?.* Clementine's immediate thought was that she had to get rid of two now, and not just one. *That's a bother*, she thought, *I didn't expect this. I need to rethink my plans.*

The mood was a rather weird one at the dinner table. Clementine couldn't take her eyes off Grace who indeed looked just like her mother. Same cheap make-up, same bright red lipstick and dark eyes, same cheap perfume. It was so eerie.

"You know, Grace, Rosina spoke of a brother that had died, but I don't understand why she never mentioned you."

"Oh Frank," she said. "I was taken into care just after he died. My mother couldn't cope, she was finding life very difficult. I managed to find Rosina just before I went to New Zealand. I lived with a lovely foster family and they never said a bad word about my mother. We met up just before I left England and I'm afraid we didn't quite hit it off. I'm sorry to say this to you, Frank, but Rosina was a horrible person, she was a very cold woman."

"Why do you say that?" he said. "She was a kind-hearted lady and I loved her. You only knew her for five minutes."

Grace knew that she had insulted Frank by tarnishing Rosina's memory but that's exactly how she felt. She continued, "You know, Frank, Rosina was born with a lot of my father's traits. He was a nasty, violent man who never gave a thought to anyone but himself and I'm afraid she showed a lot of those traits when I met her. She didn't want to know me and was rather offensive about me and my foster family. I've got to disagree with you there, Frank, she was a horrible individual."

"Then why did you come here to see us?" he asked. "After what you've just said that doesn't make any sense."

"Well, maybe so, but she was still my flesh and blood, still my twin sister. I wanted to meet you and Clementine, and I'm glad I did. Now if that invitation to stay is still there, I would like to stay and get to know the both of you. I'm only here for a few weeks, but I will understand if you would rather I left." Grace stood up from the table and walked towards the hall to get her coat.

"*No*, Frank said. "Please stay with us. I would like to get to know you better, you are family after all."

"Very well," she said. "I will stay."

Oh Shit! thought Clementine. *What the hell am I going to do now?*

Over the next few days Clementine's father was like a new man, laughing and joking and embracing life again. He looked so very happy. He and Grace were getting on like a house on fire. "Oh Grace, you make me feel so alive. You're a breath of fresh air!."

"Thank you," she said. "That's a lovely thing to say. I must admit you make me feel the same. I lost my poor Albert four years ago, and it can be a lonely life. You've made me feel alive again too. Thank you, Frank."

Clementine couldn't believe what she was watching. Oh hell, don't tell me this is going to be the romance of the century!. Surely not! Shortly after, Clementine came home from work and the house was empty. "Father," she shouted. "Are you there?" No reply, *I wonder where he is,* she thought. *He's always here. Oh well,* Clementine started to prepare her evening meal. She was walking upstairs to take her coat off when she heard the sound of voices coming from her father's room. Oh no, no, no, no. Clementine slowly opened her father's door, and there he was in all his glory with Grace beside him in bed. Clementine quickly closed the door and ran downstairs. "Dirty bastard!" she shouted. "You dirty bastard!"

Her father called to her, "Oh Clementine, I'm sorry. We couldn't help it, we're in love. I know it sounds terrible, I know it's just a few weeks since your mother died, but that's how it is, we love one another. Grace is going to be staying here, she's not going back to New Zealand."

"How could you, Father, I will never forgive you for this, never. My poor mother not long in her grave and there you are upstairs with of all people my *aunt*. Have you no shame? I will never forgive you — never." Clementine stormed out of the house and made her way down to her hideaway the only place she felt safe. *I can think there, I'll know what to do,* she thought. Clementine slept there that night, it didn't bother her that she was in the middle of the woods with no noises to hear but the sounds of the animals, she liked that.

She made her way to the house in the morning, thinking about what she was going to do now. Clementine packed a suitcase and left the family home, the home that she thought she would be living in but now things had all changed. She decided to book in to a local bed and breakfast. Mrs McMeikle had run the bed and breakfast since Clementine was a child, and was a lovely elderly lady who always had a smell of freshly baked scones. Clementine rang the bell and she could smell Mrs McMeikle before she could see her. "Good morning, Clementine, how can I help you?"

"Hi, Mrs McMeikle, would it be possible to book in for a few days. We are having some work carried out at the house and I just need somewhere to stay until its finished."

"Of course," she said. "If you just sign the book I will give you my loveliest room. It has a beautiful view of the woodland walk. Have you been there, Clementine?"

"Oh yes," she said. "Indeed I have."

"I don't know if you remember, Clementine, but there was the terrible disappearance of the two women a few years back, they never found them. It has never stopped people from going there though. I don't go there on my own of course but I've seen people who do. It is beautiful there."

Clementine took her case into the room and could see the view of the woodland walk from her window. "Oh, this is lovely, Mrs McMeikle, just lovely. Thank you." The time spent at the B&B gave Clementine the opportunity to sit and plan how she was going to get rid of her father and Grace. Her previous plan had just crumbled in front of her so she had to think of something else, and quick!

And of course the most amazing thing about

Clementine was her ability to read people's minds and she knew that deep down, Grace didn't love her father, she just wanted a free meal ticket while she was staying in England. Grace thought there was money to be had, the cottage with no mortgage and of course her father's pension. So all of her shit was just that — pure *shit*. Nothing was true, everything was a lie so she could justify the demise of Grace and her father no problem. She had a reason as to why they both should die and she was at peace with that. Clementine sat that evening in her hideaway thinking how she was going to carry out the deed.

But very soon any plans she had thought of would be taken out of her hands. Grace and her father summoned her to the cottage to tell her some news. "Why do you need to speak to me, Father?" she said.

"Clementine, I have some very important news for you. I have decided to go to New Zealand with Grace. I'm really sorry I've got to leave you, but I have myself to think about now, and a new life with a new woman is just what the doctor ordered."

"*Well*! she said. "Thanks for that, Father, thanks for fucking off to another country and just leaving me here to get on with it."

"I'm really sorry, Clementine, but I've got myself to think about. You're an adult, you will be absolutely fine. The house is yours now, and you don't have to worry about me."

Clementine thought for a minute, *mmmm well, maybe so, but I'm still angry, Father. Christ, have I got this all wrong,* she thought. She was so sure Grace was after her father's money but now... She wasn't so sure.

Grace cleared her throat and began to speak. "Frank, my darling, I don't mean to cause any trouble, but you will need the money from the sale of the house when we move to New Zealand."

"Oh God, I hadn't thought of that, darling. Of course we will. Sorry, Clementine, the house will need to go up for sale. You understand don't you?"

Clementine looked at her father with such hatred but managed a tight, false smile. "Of course you do, Father. Of course you do. Don't worry about me, I will be fine. I just need time to find somewhere else to live, after all this is my home. The place I have lived all of my life."

"Of course, Clementine," he said. "We can help you look, if you like?"

"Oh, no thank you, Father," she sneered. "I will be fine. If you will excuse me, Father," she paused, "And Grace, I will be on my way. Talk to you later."

"Oh, OK," her father said. "See you later."

Clementine felt a rage inside her like no other. The anger was all consuming. She was scaring herself with the way she was feeling and just how upsetting this was for her. *People just don't realise that when I get angry, people get hurt or even die*, she thought. *For God's sake you would think that they would have more sense. People incense me, people enrage me and people just piss me off!* They were a rare breed and this situation just reminded her of why she didn't socialise with other human beings, why she liked her own company, and more importantly why she was so very much better than them.

Grace continued to piss Clementine off when she was

living at 'her home' acting as if she had lived there for years! Cheek! Things were a bit tense in the family home (well, that's putting it mildly!) when one day her father received a phone call from the estate agent in the village.

"I have some news," her father announced. "Someone wants to buy the cottage, warts and all!" He laughed excitedly at the thought of the money he was going to get and his new life in New Zealand. Not a single thought for Clementine.

"Oh Father, I'm so pleased for you," she said through gritted teeth. "How wonderful." Clementine looked over and there was Grace all over her father like some cheap tart. *I can't take this anymore*, she thought, *I need to do something this evening. But what?* She hadn't been able to come up with anything 'suitable' for her father and Grace. *Think Clementine, think!*

Clementine looked round, and there was the bold Grace standing in the lounge!! *Cheek!* she thought. "Hello Grace, I thought you were in bed?"

"Well clearly not, my dear. I need to have a quiet chat with you, woman to woman." Grace sat down next to Clementine, placing her hand on her shoulder. "Now, my dear, we seem to have a slight problem."

"Really? What's that," said Clementine.

"Well, my dear, I have the same gift as you. I also can read people's minds and I have, it has to be said, 'got rid of' people who have stood in my way over the years. Do you know what I mean?" she said very quietly.

Clementine looked at her and Grace had the same menacing and evil look Clementine had saw in herself. Suddenly Clementine became very anxious and scared.

"Now, my dear, let me make myself perfectly clear. Your father and I, *are* going to New Zealand, the house is being sold, and lastly, you, my dear, will most definitely not be standing in our way. Do I make myself clear?"

Clementine stared at her, those cold eyes, those tight lips and those gritted teeth. All the signs she had seen in herself. "Yes," said Clementine. "Crystal clear."

"Just remember, Clementine, I can make you disappear, and no one would ever find you. So you be a good girl, and do as I am saying, and we will all be happy. OK, my dear."

"You're a fucking nutcase," Clementine said.

"Thank you, Clementine, thanks for that compliment, but of course, remember we are both fucking nutcases." She laughed loudly as she stood up to leave the room.

"Oh by the way, Clementine, do you remember my younger brother who died? I don't know if you had heard about him. Always such a sickly boy. From the moment I met him I despised him, always coughing and spluttering, spreading his germs all over the place. And always so unwell, causing such a bother in our family. Well my dear, a lovely soft pillow helped him along his final journey. Ever so gently placed over his sickly, pale, ugly face. And what a relief for my mother when he died. I knew that she would be upset, I could see that but I knew that one day she would thank me. She wouldn't be so tied to him if he were gone. She could have some freedom again. We could go out for walks and have our chats, you know, the ones we had before the brat came along and ruined it for us? So, think on, Clementine. You really don't want to upset your mad, bad, Aunt Grace.

Clementine began to tremble. *Oh my god. She's crazy,*

I'm not like that. I'm nothing like her. Stupid cow!

Clementine lay in her bed thinking of the challenge that lay ahead. *Oh Aunt Grace may think she has outwitted me, but she's in for a shock*, she thought. *This is my home and there is no way she is selling it! No way!* She couldn't sleep, her mind was racing and her heart was beating so loud and fast she thought it would burst. Clementine lifted a pillow from her bed and quietly crept to her father's bedroom. Her plan? Simply to kill Grace and her father. Her hand reached for the handle of the bedroom door. She quietly opened the door and walked over to her father. She could see the dark silhouette. The moon shining through the curtains and casting a very faint light on his body. Grace was on the other side of the bed. She could see the top of her head. Clementine looked at her father. He looked so still, so peaceful... She held the pillow with two hands and suddenly stopped. *There's something not right here*, she thought. She looked at her father who appeared *very* pale and *very* still. She touched him and he felt slightly cold. *Oh my God, he's dead!*

She slowly looked round at Grace, who had managed to sit up in bed without making a noise. Clementine's throat was dry, her eyes fixed on Grace and she had an overwhelming feeling of pure dread. "Clementine, my dear, you're too late. He's gone, I just couldn't resist. It's in the blood, you know." She smiled and slowly got out of bed. She walked over to Clementine and took the pillow from her hands. "Do sit down, dear, you must be in shock. After all, he is your father but more importantly, and if truth be told, 'selfishly' unfortunately he's the father of my eldest child. The child was born when I was a teenager. It was just when I had begun to see your mother again, and I met him one evening when they were out for a drink. Your mother was quite drunk that evening and when he dropped her off, he offered to walk me home.

"I didn't think anything of it. Why would I? A mere child myself. He was rather brutal in his attack I'm afraid, dear. Quite brutal and quite vicious. He not only raped me, he beat me as well. I'm not quite sure where all that anger came from."

"What!" said Clementine. "No way, you're lying, he would never have done any of those things."

"No, my dear, I'm afraid not. I've got absolutely no reason to lie. And I'm sorry to say that even after all these years he had no recollection of the event, well either that, or he thought it was so insignificant. Either way I find that quite unforgivable. It epitomises the kind of man he was. My life was never the same after that. He took my heart and soul that night and didn't give his brutal act, or indeed the aftermath of such an act, a second thought. They were a very suited couple when you think of it, Clementine. Selfish, brutal and evil."

"And what of you?" roared Clementine. "You murdered your own brother for God's sake! What does that say about you?"

"True, my dear, true, but you're not really so very different from me. If truth be told, you're a killer just like me. We are one and the same."

"Never! Never"! shouted Clementine. "And what are you going to do now, Aunt Grace? Kill me? Is that the next move in your evil and wicked plan?"

"Oh no, my dear. Not at all. I didn't plan to kill him this

evening, but he was lying in bed next to me, and the urge to kill him quite simply just took over. I couldn't help myself. You know that feeling, Clementine? Oh but dear, what are we going to do now?"

"*We*! What's with the '*we*'?"

"Well, I do need your help, my dear. I need to get rid of the body. Any ideas Clementine?"

"Oh, my God!! You are asking me to help get rid of my father's body."

"Well of course, my dear, that's what you're good at. Be honest, Clementine, you excel in the subject of getting rid of trash." She laughed loudly. "Now come on, dear, where can we take him? I simply don't know this neck of the woods, so I would appreciate your help, if you don't mind.

"Aunt Grace, you're not asking for a cup of tea, for Christ's sake! You're asking me to help get rid of my father's body."

"Ooohh, I know, my dear, exciting isn't it?"

Clementine looked at her and they both began to laugh. Clementine had to admit they were both so alike and a part of her enjoyed the excitement of 'body binning'.

"Okay, Aunt Grace, I know where we can take him. We could take him to the cellar. There's a narrow old bricked passageway that was never used, we could slide him in there."

"That sounds ideal, my dear, just ideal."

Clementine and Aunt Grace lifted her father from his bed, one at one end and one at the other. They gently walked down the two flights of stairs and in the dim light of the cellar laid him on the ground. Clementine held both his feet and simply slid him into the passageway as far as she could push him. She stood up and looked around at her Aunt Grace. All Clementine could see were the whites of her teeth and the whites of her eyes. Her eyes narrowed with an evil look like no other. "Clementine, I've got it all planned. What we can do, is ask for the money from the sale of the house to be transferred into mine and your father's bank account. We opened it a couple of weeks ago. No one will even ask where he is because everyone knew we were going to New Zealand."

"Oh, my God, Aunt Grace, that sounds simply perfect, I can't wait. But what about me Aunt Grace? They may ask about me?"

"Oh honestly, Clementine! Do you think they will? Those narrow-minded villagers? They don't give a shit about you, all they care about is themselves."

"True." She chuckled. "Very true."

They both returned to the house and began to pack their bags. "Are you ready?" Aunt Grace roared. "We need to go, my sweet." Clementine walked into the lounge and the atmosphere had changed somewhat. She felt very uneasy and very, very scared. Now, now, Clementine, come in. This is your home after all. Let's have a drink before we go."

"Eh," she stuttered. "No thanks, Aunt Grace, I don't drink."

"Oh, come on now! Have a small sherry with me. Why are you afraid, Clementine?"

"I don't know. I just don't feel that things are right. I'm not very good at trusting people."

"Oh, come on now, my dear, it's me, your Aunt Grace. Have a sip."

"Well, OK," she said. "Because it's you. Clementine very slowly sipped a little of the sherry, looking intently at her aunt. A sense of relief came over Clementine as she sipped the sweet bitter drink. "Oh, that tastes really nice, Aunt Grace."

"There, there, my dear Clementine, did you think I was going to hurt you? You are me, and I am you. We are reunited souls. Now let's get ready and leave for the airport. The taxi is on its way, there's nothing left for us here. Oh, and by the way, Clementine, there is something I want you to help me with when we get to New Zealand."

"Really? What's that, Aunt Grace?

Grace grinned. "Well my dear, there's a piece of trash that's living in my home. I need it to go."

"Out to the bin, Aunt Grace?"

"Exactly, my dear, out with the goddamned rubbish!" They both laughed hysterically.

Then both ladies looked at one another, their eyes locked, knowing what one another were thinking. Pure evil seeped from every pore of their bodies and Clementine knew she had met her soulmate, her partner in crime, her confidante.

The two ladies left in their taxi for the airport. The quiet picturesque cottage, sitting still in the beautiful tranquil background of the night. And in the quiet dead of night, the faint sound of blood-curdling screams could be heard coming from the cellar.